Sir William
and the
Pumpkin Monster

SIR WILLIAM

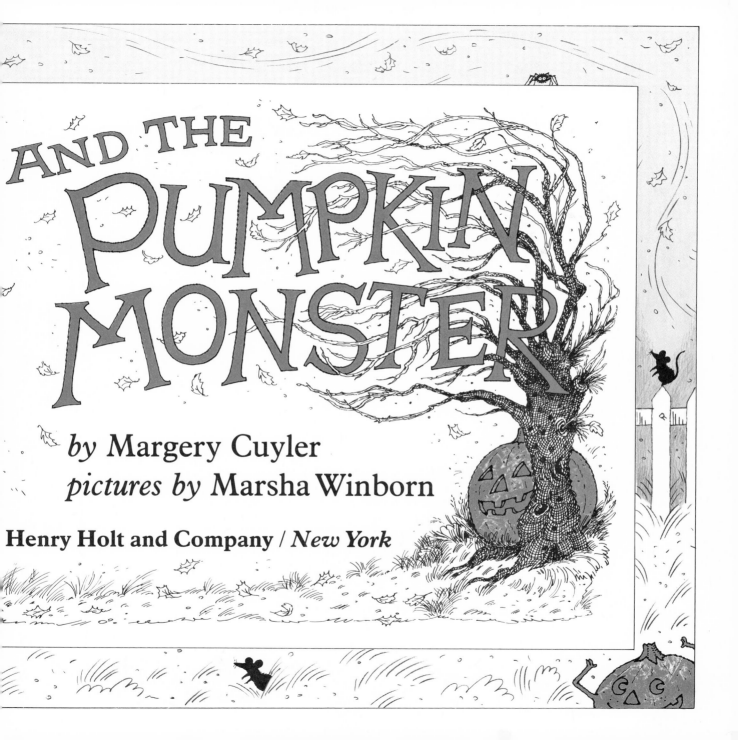

AND THE PUMPKIN MONSTER

by **Margery Cuyler**
pictures by **Marsha Winborn**

Henry Holt and Company / *New York*

Published by Henry Holt and Company, Inc.,
115 West 18th Street, New York, New York 10011.
Published in Canada by Fitzhenry & Whiteside Limited,
195 Allstate Parkway, Markham, Ontario L3R 4T8.

Library of Congress Cataloging in Publication Data
Cuyler, Margery.
    Sir William and the pumpkin monster.
    Summary: Unsuccessful in his schemes to frighten the
family he lives with, a frustrated ghost has a terrifying
experience himself on Halloween night.
    [1. Ghosts—Fiction.   2. Halloween—Fiction]
I. Winborn, Marsha, ill.   II. Title.
PZ7.C997Si   1984   [E]   84-610
ISBN: 0-8050-0247-2 (hardcover)
10   9   8   7   6   5   4   3

ISBN: 0-8050-1017-3 (paperback)
10   9   8   7   6   5   4   3   2   1

Henry Holt books are available at special discounts
for bulk purchases for sales promotions, premiums,
fund-raising, or educational use. Special editions
or book excerpts can also be created to specification.

        For details, contact:

        Special Sales Director
        Henry Holt & Co., Inc.
        115 West 18th Street
        New York, New York 10011

Printed in the United States of America

First published in hardcover by Henry Holt and Company,
Inc., in 1984
First Owlet edition 1989

For Jamie   M.C.

To October 31   M.W.

Lucky Sir William.
He haunted the Nevilles' house.
Unlike other people, who fainted and screamed
when they saw him, the Nevilles thought
he was wonderful.

When Mr. Neville practiced the piano, Sir William
turned the pages of his music.

When Mrs. Neville worked in the garden,
Sir William helped her water the plants.

When Jonathan and Veronica Neville got home from school each day, Sir William played hide-and-go-seek with them.

And every afternoon, Sir William fed the Nevilles'
animals: their dog, Montague; their cat, Geranium;
and their parrot, Priscilla.

Indeed, the Nevilles could not imagine life without
Sir William.

One day in late October, Sir William woke up thinking, "I don't want to turn the pages of Mr. Neville's music or water Mrs. Neville's plants or play with the Neville children or feed the Neville pets anymore. I want to make them faint and lose their hair and feel the cold touch of my spidery fingers on their flesh. I want them to be scared of me. And Halloween is a good time to start."

On Halloween morning, Sir William attached a ball and chain to his leg and clanked his way to the dining room. Then he hid under the table. When the Neville family sat down for breakfast, Sir William rattled his ball and chain. Mrs. Neville peered below.

"Why, Sir William," she said, "what are you doing down there? Stop making such a racket. It's breakfast time."

Sir William stood up and shook his ball and chain again.

"Are you feeling unwell?" asked Mr. Neville.

"Unwell, indeed," muttered Sir William as he disappeared through the dining room wall.

Geranium was sunning herself in front of the sitting room window. Sir William tiptoed up to her and shouted "BOOOOO!" Geranium opened one eye, then shut it again.

"Impossible cat," said Sir William. "Doesn't she know a scary ghost when she sees one?"

"Sees one, sees one," echoed Priscilla from her perch.

"Oh, be quiet," snapped Sir William as he passed through the wall to the garden.

PSSSST! KITTY KITTY.....

Sir William sat in the pumpkin patch, trying to think of something else to do. Then he remembered the skeleton in the town museum. He jumped on Mr. Neville's bicycle and pedaled as fast as he could into town. He ran up to the science room in the museum and stole the skeleton from its case. Then he tucked it under his arm and bicycled back to the Nevilles' house.

Many people screamed and fainted when they saw
Sir William, but he didn't notice. He was too busy
thinking about what he was going to do next.

When he got home, he sat the skeleton in the chair near Mr. Neville's piano.

"Oh, there you are, Sir William," said Mr. Neville, entering the room for his morning practice. "I've been looking all over for you."

Sir William shook the skeleton so that its bones clicked and clacked.

"Really, Sir William. You look ridiculous playing with that skeleton. Why don't you give it to Montague? He loves to gnaw on bones."

"You just don't appreciate a scary skeleton when you see one," grumbled Sir William. He clambered up to the attic, where he spent the rest of the day trying to think up a way to scare the Neville children. Finally, he thought of one.

When it was dark, he raided all the closets in the house. He put on a wig of scraggly hair and painted his fingernails black. Then he dressed up in a ragged gown that had belonged to Mrs. Neville's great aunt Agatha. He took a broom from the pantry closet and tiptoed out into the chilly night. The moon was full, and trick-or-treaters were walking up and down the street.

Sir William hid behind some bushes, waiting for Jonathan and Veronica to walk by in their Halloween costumes. As soon as he saw them coming, he leapt in front of them and screamed, "HAIL-AH-KEZAC, ABRACADACK, I'M A WITCH, THINK OF THAT!"

"Why, it's Sir William," said Jonathan, who was dressed up as a pirate.

"You look silly," said Veronica from inside her bat costume. "You should be home in bed."

"In bed!" shouted Sir William. "That's no place for a ghost on Halloween."

"Yes, it is," said Veronica. "You know you shouldn't be out scaring little kids."

"That's what you think!" said Sir William. "But you haven't seen the last of me yet!"

"Silly children," he muttered, as he stomped down the street. "I'll show them!" But as he turned the corner, he came face to face with an enormous monster. It had a huge pumpkin head with fiery eyes and jagged teeth. It had eight paws and strange, feathery hair. "Yeowwwwwwwwwwww," it screeched.

Sir William screamed and fainted as the pumpkin monster jumped over him and collided with Jonathan and Veronica.

When the children and animals got all sorted
out, they helped Sir William to his feet.

"We hope you'll stay home on Halloween
from now on," said Veronica.

"We like you just the way you are," added
Jonathan.

"Acting scary is hard work," said Sir William.
"I need to go to bed."

From then on, everyone except Jonathan and Veronica spent Halloween in the Nevilles' house. Mr. Neville practiced on his piano. Mrs. Neville watered her plants. Montague chewed on bones. Geranium and Priscilla slept.

And Sir William gave out candy to all the children who came to the house to trick-or-treat.

THE END